This Book Belongs to:

THE MIGHTY

GEORGE THE GALLANT

ANNABEL THE BRAVE

SCARLET THE DRAGON

VICTOR THE VALIANT

"To the beautiful ladies in my life—my wife, Elle, and my daughter, Lucia—with love, xxx" —Pan Georgiou

Written by Rosa Foy

Illustrated by Pantelis Georgiou

This edition first published in 2020 by IG Design Group Americas, Inc.
©IG Design Group Americas, Inc., Atlanta, Georgia.

Published by IG Design Group Americas, Inc., Atlanta, GA 30342

THE Scarlet DRAGON

VICTOR the VALIANT

Someday, thought Sir George the Gallant, I will be dubbed Hero of Wintamere. My portrait will hang in the Great Hall right next to my great-grandfather Victor the Valiant. All I have to do is fend off a fierce—

"GEORGE!" Master Bruno snapped George out of his thoughts. "You will not defeat a dragon by dreaming."

George knew his teacher was right. So George practiced his sword-fighting and fire-dodging.

He repeated his courageous mantras. "I am a brave hero!" said George. "I am not afraid of ferocious dragons."

George had been training to fight dragons his whole life. But he had never seen one before. As he walked home that day, George heard the villagers talking.

"Something spooked my horse this morning," said one man. "It ran and hid in a pile of straw."

"The vegetables in my garden were eaten, and the leaves were burnt to a crisp," said another.

A woman cried out, "I saw it myself! A scarlet-red streak through the sky."

A spooked horse? Fire? A streak through the sky? George was sure this could only mean one thing. He went home and climbed up onto his roof to look for a dragon.

While George was gazing into the bright blue sky, a messenger approached on his horse. "Sir George!" the messenger called out. "King Albert has requested your presence at the royal palace."

"Me?" George said. "But I am just a boy."

"The king does not tell me his business, only who to call before him," said the messenger. A royal warrant had been unrolled and was hanging from the messenger's hand.

George felt his heart leap. He scrambled down from the roof and jumped onto his noble steed, Johnny Runs-a-Lot. Johnny felt George's excitement and galloped as fast as he could.

An hour later, George saw the majestic castle on the horizon. He admired its beauty, with turrets atop the corner towers and a drawbridge stretching over a teal-green moat.

"Sir George the Gallant, at your service," he said as he bowed before the king.

"The time has come for you to be a hero like your great-grandfather," King Albert said. "Sir George, there is a dragon on the loose. I ask you to defend Wintamere and save its people from this fearsome red beast! And if you are successful, your bravery will be rewarded."

ALEX THE MIGHTY

JACK THE GIANT

LUCIA THE LITTLEST

George was ready to set off on his journey, but first he needed to find the dragon. So he climbed the Wintamere watchtower and called out,

"COME OUT AND FIGHT, FOUL BEAST!"

George waited. He tried to prepare himself by practicing his sword-fighting and fire-dodging moves. Then he wondered if the dragon was very big. Or very fiery. George nervously mumbled to himself, "I am a brave hero. I am not afraid of—

Suddenly, George saw a red streak in the sky. He pulled out his sword, but instead of fighting, the dragon yelped. A small puff of smoke came out of its nose, and it quickly flew away.

George scratched his head. This wasn't quite what he had practiced for. But he didn't want to miss his chance. He hopped onto his horse, Johnny, and galloped after the dragon.

George followed the dragon all the way out of the village
until finally it swooped down into a cave.

George hopped off his horse and approached the cave
entrance. He was ready to call for the dragon to come
out when he heard loud sniffling coming from inside.

George tiptoed into the cave, hiding in the shadows. Snap! George stepped on a stick. The dragon jumped and quickly hid behind a boulder.

This is it! thought George, gripping his sword. *The dragon is cornered. This is my chance to become a hero.*

But then George noticed the dragon's tail peeking out from behind the boulder. It was trembling.

"Wait, is a dragon really afraid of me?" asked George.

The dragon whimpered.

George sighed.
"You can come out.
I won't hurt you."

Slowly, the dragon poked its head out from
behind the boulder. It watched George set down
his sword. "I'm sorry for scaring your village," said the
dragon. "It's just that so much of the forest has been cut
down that it's the only place to get food."

"Why don't you just ask for some food, then?" George inquired.

"Are you kidding? I'm the Scarlet Dragon!" she said. "All people fear me, and all knights want to fight me so they can be called a hero."

George blushed. Then he pulled a sandwich out of his sack and broke it in two.

As George and Scarlet ate together, they tried to think of what to do. They talked about all the different ways the dragon could help the people of Wintamere. Then George had an idea.

"I've got it!" George said at last. "Come with me to Wintamere. No one will hurt you, I promise."

And with that, Scarlet decided to trust her new friend, and she followed Sir George back to the village.

When they arrived at George's home, he told Scarlet to hide behind his house. "You can do this," he told the dragon. "Just tell yourself, 'I am a brave hero.'"

George gathered the villagers together. "I have brought a powerful but kind friend to meet you," he said. "She is here to help us. So from now on, there is no reason to be afraid."

Then he called to his friend. The crowd gasped
as the Scarlet Dragon appeared before them.
"Meet the new defender of Wintamere."

From that day on, the Scarlet Dragon flew above Wintamere, watching over the village. And every day she visited the watchtower, where her friend George brought a dozen sandwiches to share.

One morning, King Albert called the two of them to his castle. "George, you may not have defeated the dragon, but what you did was even better," he said. "Sir George the Gallant, I dub you Hero of Wintamere."

Then he asked Scarlet to bow her head. "And, Dragon, it is my pleasure to dub you Dame Scarlet, brave Defender of Wintamere."

From that day on, in the Great Hall beside George's great-grandfather hung a portrait of not one but two heroes.

JOSH THE JOLLY

EMILY THE ELEGANT

RALPH THE NOBLE

LAUREN THE GREAT

LUCIA THE LITTLEST

JACK THE GIANT

MEGAN THE MAGNIFICENT

HOLLY THE CONQUEROR

The End